IN MEMORY OF AMY KROUSE ROSENTHAL

CLARION BOOKS IS AN IMPRINT OF HARPERCOLLINS PUBLISHERS.

THE UMBRELLA

TEXT COPYRIGHT © 2023 BY BETH FERRY

ILLUSTRATIONS COPYRIGHT © 2023 BY TOM LICHTENHELD

FOR INFORMATION ABOUT PERMISSION TO

REPRODUCE SELECTIONS FROM THIS BOOK, WRITE TO

PERMISSIONS, HARPERCOLLINS PUBLISHING,

195 BROADWAY, NEW YORK, NEW YORK 10007.

WWW.HARPERCOLLINSCHILDRENS.COM

ISBN 978-0-35-844772-6

TYPOGRAPHY BY WHITNEY LEADER-PICONE

THE ILLUSTRATIONS WERE DONE IN PENCIL AND WATERCOLOR

ON STONEHENGE PAPER,

WITH A BIT OF PHOTOSHOP TO PUT IT ALL TOGETHER.

23 24 25 26 27 RTLO 10 9 8 7 6 5 4 3 2 1 · FIRST EDITION

The Umbrella

by Beth Ferry and Tom Lichtenheld

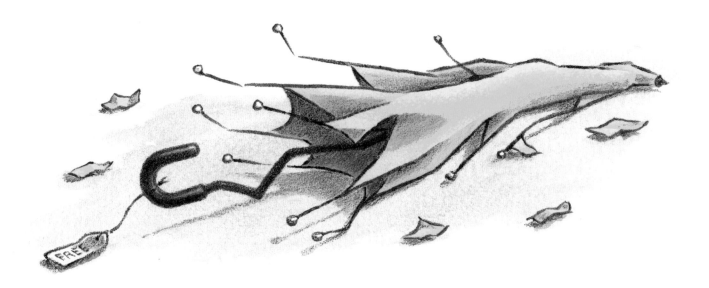

CLARION BOOKS | *An Imprint of HarperCollinsPublishers*

Dreary.

Weary.

Drip.

Drop.

Nonstop.

Gotta go—

rain or snow.

Stop.

Stare.

Gotta wonder...

What's
in there?

Hat?

Bat?

What is
that?

Coat?

Boat?

Read the note.

Come on, pup.

She'll wrap it up!

Dashing.

Splashing.

Pitter-patters.

Crumble.

Tumble.

Trail of tatters.

Mad!

Sad.

Too bad.

Come on, pup.

Snuggle up.

Nights and days.

Always grays.

Drip.   Drop.   Nonstop.

Come on, pup.

Hurry up!

Hey, that's new.

Something grew!

Come on, pup.

Dig them up!

To the square.
Gotta share!

Bright umbrellas
everywhere.

Goodbye, dreary.
Goodbye, gray.

We just chased the
clouds away.

Now we're off
to chase the sun.

Something
splendid
has begun.

Watch as sun-filled
days unfurl.

All because of
one bright girl.